The Adventure of Ari and Tacari

PAGE PUBLISHING, INC.
New York, NY

First originally published by Page Publishing, Inc. 2019

ISBN 978-1-64350-742-2 (Hardcover)
ISBN 978-1-64350-741-5 (Digital)

Printed in the United States of America

The Adventure of

Ari and Tacari

The Subway

Written by Lanita Philmore

Ari and Tacari, two cool cats
A couple of blackbirds with funny hats
One wears glasses that have no lenses
The other wears a top hat that comes to a bend
They live in the city downtown Philly
In a shoebox apartment that's itty-bitty
These two birds are peas in a pod

Enjoy walking more than flying
Do you think that is odd?
Every day is an adventure up- or downtown
Only if you see Ari and Tacari around
They love field trips
And learning new tricks
One thinks very quick
And the other is full of wit

There are tales to tell for days on end
They find more trouble than they should
It never ends
So I'll begin the fun
With adventure number one
Ari and Tacari had just moved to town
And they both needed jobs
So they could settle down

Early one morning, they woke up and yawned
Threw on their clothes and started moving
The day along

They decided to take the subway
What a way to start a first day
Never had they been there before
Neither knew what was in store

Ari said, "Let's take the elevator down."
Tacari replied, "Look. It's broken." So they frown
Do remember these birds don't fly
They started down the stairs
With a great big sigh
One hour later, they met their train
Stepping inside, they scratched their brains

Ari complained, "I see no birds."
Tacari replied, laughing, "This is different herd.
We are among people, humans if you will.
Yes, we should have brought jackets.

I'm catching a chill."
"The train is moving!" Tacari shouted
"But where are we going?
There's only one routed."

Ari asked, "What does the sign say?"
Tacari replied, "Too far up to say.
We'll have to use good judgement,
For time is our friend.

If we ride too long,
We will reach the end.
So we'll ride for ten minutes
And jump when we stop!
Though we must be quick. We must be safe.
Hold on to your hat, for the wind is great."

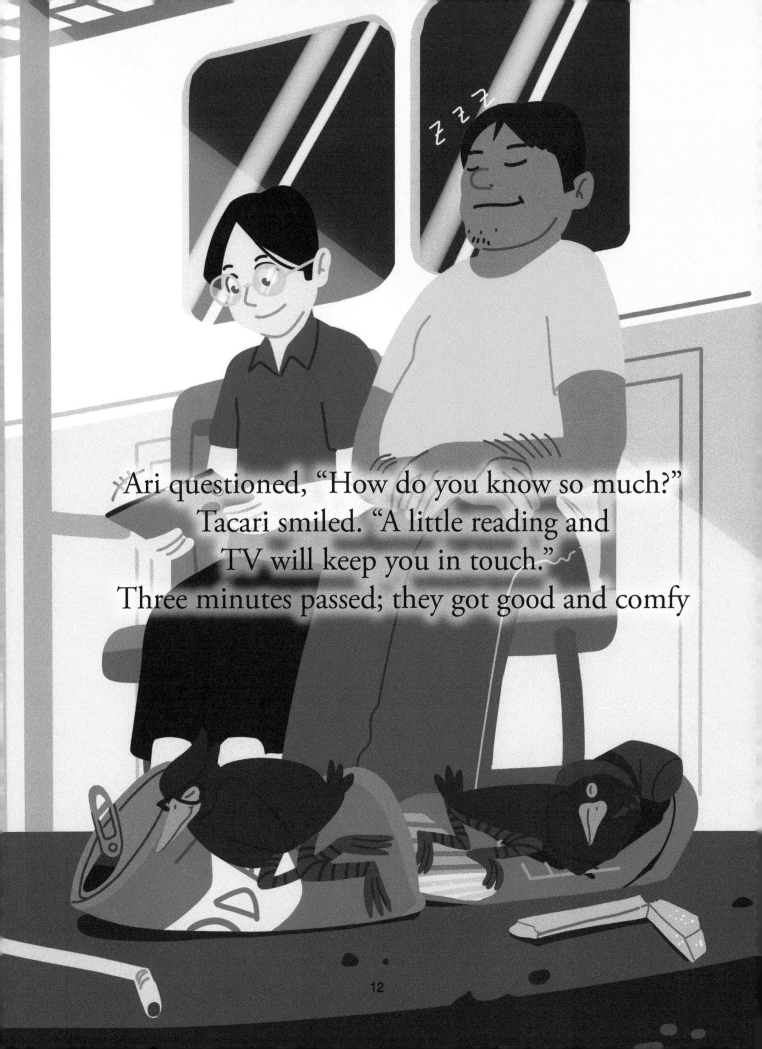

Ari questioned, "How do you know so much?"
Tacari smiled. "A little reading and
TV will keep you in touch."
Three minutes passed; they got good and comfy

They fell asleep on something hard and lumpy
Finally, they awoke from a long sleep
There was no one in sight

Nor one pair of feet
The next stop, they jumped off
and found the escalator quick
The smell of the hallway was making them sick

Came to the street and hitched
a ride on a bus or a buggy
Only two blocks from their street, how lovely
So you see, they never made it to town
They spent the whole day just lying around

About the Author

At the age of 34, Lanita Philmore is publishing her first children's book ever. Originally from North Philadelphia, born in 1983, she first began writing poetry and short stories at the age of 12. Also a working mother of three kids including a young adult, Lanita has been a teacher for over ten years to mostly young children ages 6 weeks to 12 years.

Although she went to school and received an Associates Degree in Business Management she truly enjoys writing in her spare time. Making creatures/characters come to life in funny adventures that entertain the young mind. Her love for children persuaded her to jump into writing children's stories head first with the hopes of providing books one day for children of all ages.

CPSIA information can be obtained
at www.ICGtesting.com
Printed in the USA
BVHW021318120419
545361BV00010B/22/P